Dink, Josh, and Ruth Rose aren't the only kid detectives!

What about you?

Can you find the hidden message inside this book?

There are 26 illustrations in this book, not counting the one on the title page, the map at the beginning, and the picture of the crown that repeats at the start of many of the chapters. In each of the 26 illustrations, there's a hidden letter. If you can find all the letters, you will spell out a secret message!

If you're stumped, the answer is on the bottom of page 136.

Happy detecting!

To Dr. Emily Stanley, who encouraged me to write.
For making me rewrite again and again, thank you!
—R.R.

To Norman, the biggest San Francisco Giants fan ever
—J.S.G.

Text copyright © 2011 by Ron Roy
Cover art and interior illustrations copyright © 2011 by John Steven Gurney

Visit us on the Web!
SteppingStonesBooks.com
randomhouse.com/kids

Educators and librarians, for a variety of teaching tools,
visit us at randomhouse.com/teachers

Library of Congress Cataloging-in-Publication Data
Roy, Ron.
The New Year dragon dilemma / by Ron Roy ; illustrated by John Steven Gurney.
  p. cm. — (A to Z mysteries. Super edition ; #5)
"A Stepping Stone book."
Summary: Dink, Josh, and Ruth Rose are enjoying a visit to San Francisco when Holden, their college-age tour guide, is accused of abducting Miss Chinatown from the Chinese New Year parade and stealing her valuable crown.
ISBN 978-0-375-86880-1 (trade) — ISBN 978-0-375-96880-8 (lib. bdg.) —
ISBN 978-0-375-89963-8 (ebook)
[1. Mystery and detective stories. 2. Robbers and outlaws—Fiction. 3. Chinese New Year—Fiction. 4. San Francisco (Calif.)—Fiction. 5. Chinatown (San Francisco, Calif.)—Fiction.] I. Gurney, John Steven, ill. II. Title.
PZ7.R8139New 2011
[Fic]—dc23
2011015145

Printed in the United States of America
10 9 8 7 6 5 4 3 2 1

A to Z Mysteries®

Super Edition #5

The New Year Dragon Dilemma

by Ron Roy

illustrated by
John Steven Gurney

A STEPPING STONE BOOK™

Random House 🏠 New York

GOLDEN GATE
BRIDGE

ALCATRAZ

CANADA

SAN FRANCISCO,
CALIFORNIA

GREEN LAWN,
CONNECTICUT

U S A

MEXICO

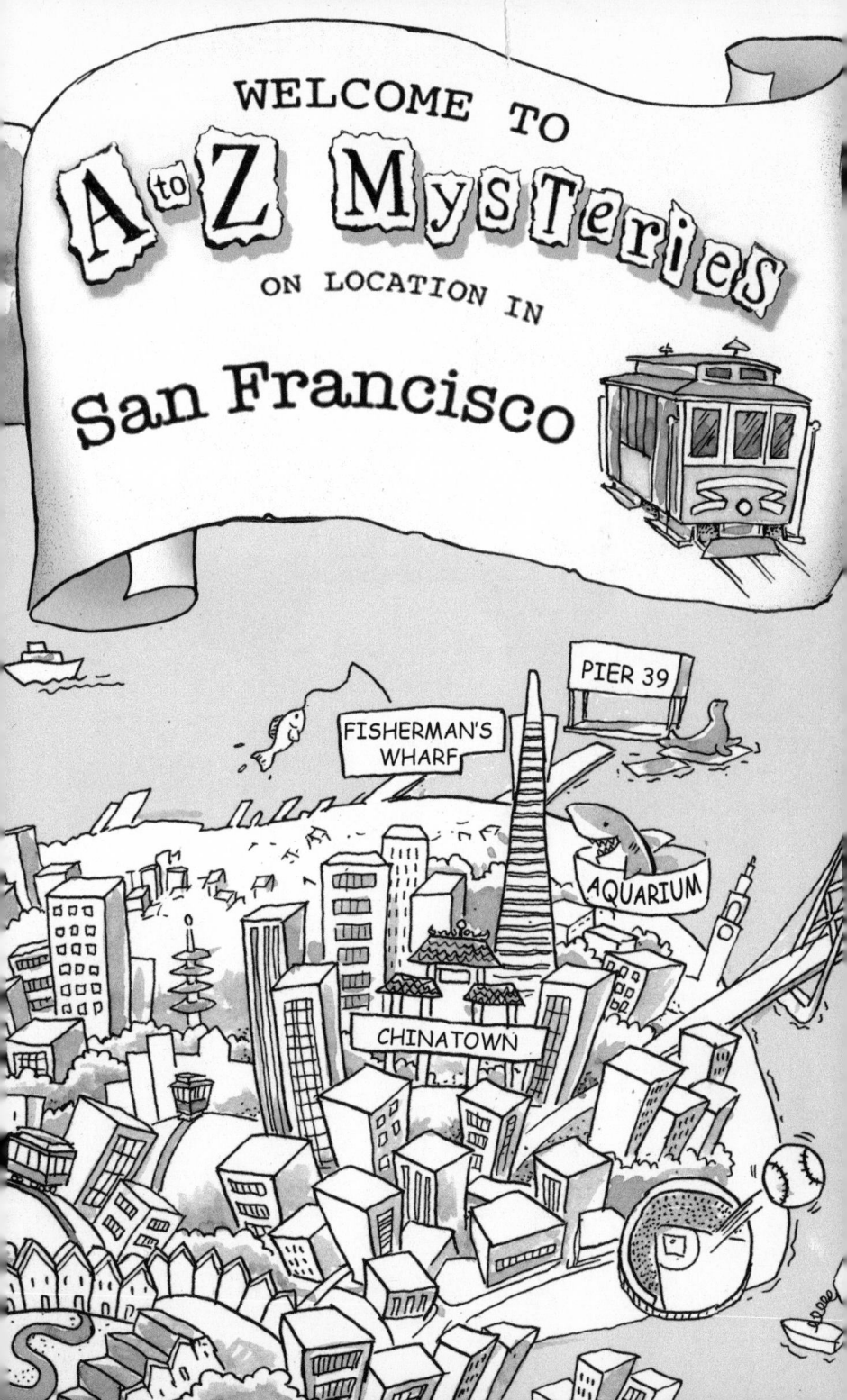

CHAPTER 1

"Holden, here we are!" Dink yelled. "Sorry we're late!"

Dink, Josh, and Ruth Rose ran toward the tall young man with black hair. It was February school break, and the kids were with Dink's father in San Francisco, California. Mr. Duncan had business meetings, and he'd brought Dink and his two best friends along. They were staying at the Bayside Hotel. The hotel was near Chinatown, where a lot of Chinese people lived and had businesses.

"Hi, guys," Holden said. Holden Wong was leaning against a three-wheeled buggy he called his Green Machine. The contraption looked like a bike, and Holden pedaled it like a bike. But there was an umbrella to keep out the rain and sun, and a narrow bench where two or three passengers could sit.

Dink's father had hired Holden to show the kids the San Francisco sights. Like Dink, Josh, and Ruth Rose, Holden was on school vacation. He was in college, studying acting. He wanted to move to Hollywood and work in the movies after he graduated.

"I like your shirt," Ruth Rose said. "We match today!"

Holden's T-shirt was lime-green. It said GREEN MACHINE on the front, with a map of San Francisco on the back. It was a cool day, and he had tied a white sweater around his waist.

Holden unlatched a small compartment under the passenger bench. He pulled out a green helmet shaped like half of an oversized lime. "I like your outfit, too," he said.

Ruth Rose liked to dress in one color. Today she had chosen green for her sweatshirt, pants, sneakers, scarf, and hat.

"Gee, Dink and I should have worn green, too," Josh said. "We'd look like a salad!" Josh carried his sketchbook and a few pencils. He wanted to be an artist when he grew up.

Dink grinned at Josh. "Not everything is about food, Josh," he said.

"Hop on," Holden said. "We're going to Fisherman's Wharf."

"What's there?" Dink asked after they sat on the bench.

"Lots of stuff," Holden said. "Fishing boats, shops, food stands, and tons of tourists!" He strapped on his helmet and pedaled into traffic.

Ruth Rose pulled a small guidebook from a pocket. "I read that there are seals at Fisherman's Wharf," she said. "Will we be able to see them?"

Holden laughed. "They're actually sea lions. You'll see them, smell them, and hear them!" he said over his shoulder.

"Cool!" Josh said. "Can I get close enough to sketch them?"

"Probably," Holden said. "But they smell so bad, you won't want to get *too* close!"

Holden pedaled along the busy streets. It was late afternoon, and the city was crowded. Everywhere the kids looked, they saw taxis, bikes, motorcycles, buses, and people. Dink saw a dog walker with six dogs on leashes! He was glad they had Holden for a guide. It would be easy to get lost

in a city as busy as San Francisco.

"Hold on!" Holden yelled over his shoulder. "Steep hill!" The street dipped down suddenly, making Dink's stomach do a little flip-flop. Far ahead, he could see the ocean.

"It's like a roller-coaster ride!" Josh cried.

The street leveled off at the bottom, and soon they arrived at Fisherman's Wharf. Holden parked his bike and everyone hopped off. Thin fog swirled around them.

"What's that honking noise?" Josh asked.

"The sea lions," Holden said. "Follow me!"

The kids gaped as they walked beside Holden. They had to dodge people buying ice cream, pretzels, and coffee from street vendors. Dink saw several jugglers and artists who sketched people for money. One man had a cat that was doing tricks.

"This is like a carnival!" Ruth Rose said.

As they walked closer to the ocean, the fog grew thicker and the sea-lion honking got louder. Dink took a deep breath, enjoying the ocean smell. Through the fog, he saw several small boats tied to moorings or the end of piers.

"I see the sea lions!" Josh said, pointing. "Let's go closer."

The kids and Holden pushed through the crowd.

"Look!" Holden said, pointing past a sign that said PIER 39.

A long pier jutted out into the water, near dozens of floating wooden docks. Dark brown sea lions had taken over the docks. Some were huge, and others were smaller and younger. They were all

covered with sleek fur. Dink could smell the animals as they barked and flapped their flippers.

"This is so amazing!" Dink said. "They don't look like they're afraid of all these people."

"They're not afraid," Holden said. "They probably think we're pretty funny-looking."

"Do they stay here all year?" Ruth Rose asked.

"Some do," Holden told her. "But a lot of them migrate to other places."

"What do they eat?" Josh asked. He had opened his sketchbook and was quickly drawing one of the larger sea lions.

"Mostly fish," Holden said. "In fact, a lot of the fishermen are mad at the sea lions, because they're both after the same fish."

"Can we feed them?" Josh asked.

Holden shook his head. "Against the law," he said, pointing to a sign on a utility pole. The sign said DO NOT FEED THE SEA LIONS. Then he pointed to a small metal box at the top of the pole. "That's a camera. They're all over the place."

"Just to stop people from giving food to the sea lions?" Ruth Rose asked.

"Nope. There are a lot of pickpockets around here, too," Holden said. "So hold on to your wallets!"

Ruth Rose pulled up the hood of her sweatshirt. "It's cold here," she said.

"Not as cold as home," Dink said. Back in Connecticut, where they lived, there was a foot of snow on the ground.

Ruth Rose picked up a flyer off the sidewalk. "Guys, there's a big parade tonight," she said. "It's for the Chinese New Year. We should go!"

"The parade is a lot of fun," Holden said. He looked at his watch. "It's two o'clock now, and the parade starts around six. I could meet you somewhere if your dad says it's okay."

"I'll ask him later," Dink said.

"Chinese New Year is huge here in San Francisco," Holden told the kids. "The parade has floats, fireworks, and an amazing dragon that's about two hundred feet long. Plus, every year, the town picks a new Miss Chinatown."

Holden pointed to a picture on the flyer. It showed a pretty Chinese girl wearing a glittering crown with a red ruby in the center. "You might get to meet Miss Chinatown tonight."

"Meet her?" Ruth Rose asked.

Holden blushed. "Yup. There are two finalists, and one of them is my girlfriend, Lily Chen."

"When does she find out if she's the winner?" Dink asked.

"She may know by now," Holden said. "They keep the girls hidden until the parade. People have been voting for weeks. For the parade, they dress the winner in a special silk robe that's a hundred years old. She'll be wearing a mask and a crown."

Holden tapped the girl's picture on the flyer. "Right in the middle of the crown is a ruby that used to be owned by some Chinese ruler," he said.

Josh grinned. "Does Lily get to keep the crown?" he asked.

Holden shook his head. "Dude, the crown isn't worth anything. But that ruby is worth about a gazillion dollars," he said. "Lily told me they strap the crown on to Miss Chinatown's head so no one can steal it. She only gets to wear it for about fifteen minutes, then it goes into a safe until next year."

Josh winked. "Where's the safe?" he whispered.

They all laughed.

"Anyway, Miss Chinatown rides on a special float," Holden went on. "During the parade, she'll take off the mask. That's the first time anyone will know which girl won. The prize is a college scholarship."

"Oooh, I hope it's Lily!" Ruth Rose said. "You must be excited."

"I guess I am," Holden said. But he didn't look it. "Actually, I'm a little worried. I haven't heard from Lily since yesterday. She promised to text or call last night, but she didn't."

"Did you try to call her?" Dink asked.

"Yup, but it goes right to voice mail,"

he said. "I tried calling her parents, but no one answers."

"You said they keep the girls hidden until the parade," Ruth Rose said. "So that's probably where she is."

"I'll bet Ruth Rose is right," Dink said. He wanted to make Holden feel better. "Maybe they took the girls' cell phones away."

Holden took a deep breath, then let it out. "Yeah," he said, staring at the sea lions. "Maybe you're right."

CHAPTER 2

A teacher led her class past the three kids and Holden. "I heard that a fifth grader fell into the shark tank and got eaten!" one of the boys said to a friend. "Isn't that cool?"

"Are there sharks out there?" Josh asked, gazing toward the ocean.

"Sure, they come to try to catch the sea lions," Holden said. "But those kids are talking about the sharks in the aquarium."

"Did they really eat a fifth grader?" Dink asked.

Holden laughed. "Nope," he said. "The sharks are fed every day, so they're not hungry."

Holden leaned past Dink and pointed toward a glass and stone building next to Pier 39. "Want to go in?" he asked.

"How much does it cost?" Dink asked.

"Don't worry, your dad bought city passes for you kids," he said, reaching into his pocket. "Museums and the aquarium are free with these passes. You can also use them on buses and the cable cars."

The kids followed Holden through the crowd. Holden showed the passes at the turnstile, and they walked inside. The first thing they saw was an escalator that carried passengers past glass tunnels filled with ocean water.

"Oh my gosh!" Josh cried. "Look!" Swimming in a water tunnel, only a few

feet from their faces, was a huge shark. Then they saw other sharks, manta rays, and a bunch of other fish.

"I hope that glass is thick!" Dink said.

The kids and Holden rode the escalator until the end. Then they did it again.

"Those sharks look hungry," Josh said. "Don't they eat the other fish?"

"The staff feeds them a lot," Holden said. "If their tummies are full, the sharks won't go after anything else."

"Speaking of full tummies," Josh said, rubbing his, "I saw a snack bar over there."

"You're hungry?" Holden asked.

"Josh is always hungry," Ruth Rose said.

"Josh, don't forget we're meeting my dad for dinner later," Dink said.

"I'm a growing boy," Josh said.

Holden took the kids to the snack

bar, and they chose a long table. In the center of the table were napkins, salt and pepper shakers, and fat bottles of ketchup and mustard.

A man wearing a T-shirt and jeans sat at the far end of the table. He was hunched over a laptop. A silvery cell phone lay next to the laptop.

Dink smiled. He pulled a small notebook and pen from his pocket. He wanted to be a writer someday, and had gotten in the habit of writing down stuff he saw.

Dink thought this man looked interesting. His head was shaved, leaving only a light fuzz of hair. His face and arms were deeply tanned. On the back of each hand was a tattoo of an *M*. The man stopped typing and cut a slice from an apple with a sharp fisherman's knife.

"Come on," Holden said. "Let's get Josh some food."

"I'll stay here," Dink said. "I'm not really hungry."

The others left, and Dink started scribbling a description of the man working at his laptop.

The man's cell phone buzzed and he picked it up. "Yo," he said into the phone.

Dink kept writing. The man looked at Dink, then turned away and lowered his voice. Dink heard him say something about a boat or goat or float. Then he said, "The second tire works." Dink wrote that down, too.

Dink snuck a peek at the laptop. He saw a picture on the screen. It was a simple drawing, like a kid would make. The drawing showed a wagon with four wheels.

The man looked at Dink again, then hit a button on the laptop keyboard. The drawing vanished. In its place was a photo of a green boat with white sails.

Just then Josh, Ruth Rose, and

Holden showed up. They were carrying a large bucket of French fries and four lemonades. They plopped everything down on the table.

"I bought fries for everyone," Holden told Dink. "Josh told me you love them."

They all began eating, reaching into the bucket and sharing the ketchup.

The tattooed man flipped his cell phone shut, tucked the laptop under his arm, and strolled away.

"What kind of meetings is your dad having?" Holden asked.

"His job is teaching teachers how to use computers in their classrooms," Dink said. "He's here to meet other teachers who do the same thing."

"Sounds interesting," Holden said.

The kids finished eating.

"Can I buy some postcards?" Ruth Rose asked Holden.

"Sure, there's a rack of cards over by

the door," Holden said. "We can stop on our way out."

They cleaned up the table and headed for the exit. "I'll wait outside," Holden said.

While Dink, Josh, and Ruth Rose were looking over the card rack, Dink glanced out the window. He saw a woman with purple hair. She was licking an ice cream cone of the same color! He noticed a teenager texting on his cell phone while munching on a hamburger.

And he saw the man who had been sitting at their table with his laptop. He was walking toward the piers. To Dink, it looked as if the man was heading right for the sea lions.

Dink picked out a postcard for his mom, showing Fisherman's Wharf. The kids went to the counter and paid for their postcards.

"I'm gonna ask Holden to let me

drive that bike thing," Josh announced
as they walked outside.

"Then I'm walking," Ruth Rose said.

"Me too!" Dink said.

Josh grinned. "Gotcha!" he said.

CHAPTER 3

Dink's father took the kids to the Happy Hamburger, around the corner from the Bayside Hotel. They all had the Happy Special, a burger on sourdough bread with thin slices of pickle.

"Holden is meeting us here to take you to the parade," Dink's father said. "I asked him to have you back at the hotel no later than ten o'clock."

"Thanks, Dad," Dink said. "Why aren't you coming with us?"

"I've been with people and computer problems all day," Mr. Duncan said.

"I need some peace and quiet. While you're at the parade, I'll put my feet up and read a good book."

Dink thought about the laptop he'd seen in the snack bar at the aquarium. "Dad, how can you draw a picture on a computer?" he asked. He told his dad and the others about the strange picture he'd seen on the laptop.

"Most computers have an art function," Mr. Duncan said. "It allows you to sketch and color. What kind of laptop did the man have?"

"I don't know," Dink said. "But it looked like a real simple drawing, like a little kid would make. There was a stick-figure person in it."

Just then Holden walked in. He was wearing his white sweater and jeans. "Hi, everyone," he said. "You kids ready?"

"Hi, Holden!" they all said.

"I'm sure that Lily will be Miss

Chinatown!" Ruth Rose said. "I just have a feeling! Did she call you yet?"

Holden shook his head. "Nope. But even if she isn't chosen, I'll still see her. We made a plan a few days ago. We're gonna meet at the dragon's head when the parade ends."

"I can't wait to see the dragon!" Dink said.

"And I can't wait to drive Holden's pedal-bike thing!" Josh said.

"No way!" Dink's father said.

"Anyway, we're walking," Holden said. "It'll be too crowded for my Green Machine."

Dink's father paid the bill, and they split up. Holden and the kids walked toward Market Street, where the parade would begin. It was getting dark, and lights were coming on in shops and restaurants.

"I read that it takes one hundred

people to carry the dragon in the parade," Ruth Rose said.

"That's right," Holden said. "Wait till you see it! Two hundred legs all dressed in red, walking along under the dragon. The thing looks like the world's longest centipede!"

The closer they got to Market Street, the more people crowded the way. Finally, at the corner of Market and Second Streets, they saw a string of parked floats. All the floats were built on flat truck beds, decorated with flowers arranged in beautiful shapes. Dink saw a tiger in a jungle, temples, forests, and famous Chinese heroes, all formed by different kinds of blossoms and greenery. The floats glowed from lights hidden among the flowers.

It was mostly dark, but the block was lit with special spotlights. The smell of tasty Chinese food filled the air.

Vendors were selling everything from food to balloons to miniature dragons. Little kids in pajamas held their parents' hands. Dink noticed a row of blue porta-potties under a tree.

"Stand here and we'll get a great view," Holden said. They were behind a four-foot-high fence that would keep people out of the path of the parade. "Everything will come right by us!" he said.

"Wow!" said Josh. "How many floats are there?"

"I don't know, but this is one of the biggest parades in the world," Holden said.

"Which float will Miss Chinatown ride on?" Ruth Rose asked.

Holden pointed to one covered in blue and white blossoms. In the center was a white swan, at least ten feet tall. "That one," he said. "She rides on the swan and throws candy to the kids."

"Cool!" Josh said. "Chocolate, I hope."

"The whole swan is made of blue and white flowers," Holden said. "Lily told me there are fifty thousand blossoms on this one float."

"Guys, look!" Dink said. Off to the side stood a huge warehouse. The doors were open, and a bunch of people were carrying the dragon outside.

"That's where they keep the dragon

all year," Holden said. "They create the floats in there, too."

The dragon was the length of five school buses. It was decorated with colored cloth, buttons, ribbons, glass beads, and all kinds of things that twinkled in the light.

"It's so pretty!" Ruth Rose said. "I thought it would be a scary dragon."

"Does it breathe fire?" Josh asked Holden.

"No, but check out the lights," Holden said. Colored wires twisted into ropes made stripes along the dragon's body. Lights were wrapped around the ropes, making all two hundred feet of the dragon's body shine.

Dink thought it looked like a giant magical puppet.

The dragon's head was taller than Holden. Its mouth was open, showing fangs and a long red tongue. Big glass eyes glistened. Two dragon horns sprouted from its head.

"We call him Gum Lung," Holden said. He laughed. "Don't ask what it means, because I don't know!"

The men and women who had brought the dragon out of the warehouse began to prepare it for the parade. Some of the people had dragon masks perched on their foreheads. All of them wore bright red pants.

"They'll climb underneath Gum Lung and walk him once the parade begins," Holden said. "First there will be fireworks, then Gum Lung comes by, then the floats will drive by. The swan float will be first, carrying Miss Chinatown."

"I'm keeping my fingers crossed that it's Lily," Ruth Rose said.

Holden smiled. "Thanks. My fingers have been crossed for a week!" he said.

Suddenly the night exploded with loud bangs. Dink ducked, not knowing what the sounds were. But then he saw an enormous blue shape twinkling in the sky.

It was the fireworks. The parade was beginning!

CHAPTER 4

Dink laughed, but he put his hands over his ears. The fireworks were loud, but all the screaming and clapping were even louder.

Dink, Josh, and Ruth Rose were squeezed together next to Holden. They were in the front of the crowd.

"Here comes the dragon!" Ruth Rose said.

Gum Lung came toward them. The one hundred men and women underneath were doing fancy steps, making the dragon appear to be dancing.

The carriers made it slither and wriggle, like a snake. Music blared from speakers.

"This is awesome!" Josh shouted into Dink's ear. "We need to get one of these dragons for Green Lawn!"

Dink smiled, thinking about the little parades he'd seen back home in Connecticut. The dragon they were watching here would hardly even fit on their Main Street.

As the dragon passed by, one of the carriers stepped out from under its belly. He ran to the front of the dragon and stuck his whole head in its mouth. Everyone laughed and cheered as the man pulled his head out and ran back to his place under the dragon.

"They do that every year to prove the dragon is happy," Holden explained. "If the dragon was angry, he'd bite the guy's head off!"

A second person with red legs ran

up and put his head in the dragon's mouth, then jogged back to his position underneath. He waved to the cheering crowd.

"You want to try that, Josh?" Dink asked.

"No way!" Josh said. "The dragon looks hungry!"

The crowd laughed as a third person
came out from underneath the dragon.
He or she was short, with a dragon mask
on. But instead of running up to the
dragon's head, this person ran toward
the back of the dragon.

A few other people noticed, too, and
started pointing and laughing.

"Bet he's heading for the porta-potty!" someone behind Dink joked. The figure disappeared in the darkness behind the dragon's tail.

The dragon passed. Then the crowd burst into cheers and applause again. "It's the Miss Chinatown float!" Ruth Rose cried.

Dink felt Josh and Ruth Rose move closer to him. His belly was up against the fence.

The swan float crept slowly forward, only a few feet at a time. Dink knew that a truck was pulling the float, but the truck's cab had also been covered in blossoms. A small hole allowed the driver to see the road.

"There she is!" someone yelled.

Miss Chinatown, dressed in a gold silk robe, stood behind the swan's head. Dink recognized the fancy clothing he'd seen on the flyer. A black sash was

wrapped around the girl's waist. A silk purse hung over her shoulder. She was wearing a white mask, with her hair tucked under a golden crown. In the center of the crown, gleaming under the lights, was a ruby the size of Dink's fist.

Miss Chinatown held on to a golden rope that came from the swan's mouth, like a horse's reins. She waved her other hand at the people.

Dink wondered if the girl wearing the mask was Lily. He turned to say something to Holden. But the person behind Dink was a woman holding the hands of her two children. Holden was nowhere to be seen.

Miss Chinatown reached into her silk bag and pulled out a handful of wrapped candies. She tossed them into the crowd. Everyone tried to catch some.

"More, more!" the crowd cried.

She threw handful after handful of

candies toward the cheering people.

"She looks so beautiful!" Ruth Rose shouted above the noise. "I hope it's Lily!"

"Me too," Dink said. "Have you seen Holden?"

"Wasn't he right behind us?" Josh asked.

"I thought he was," Dink said. "But now he's gone."

The kids turned to check the people behind them.

There were several tall men with black hair, but none was Holden.

Suddenly the festivities were interrupted with more loud bangs.

"More fireworks!" Josh yelled. "Cool!"

Everyone looked at the sky, where thousands of tiny purple lights cascaded down toward the ground. A few more fireworks exploded, and then the spectacle stopped.

Dink, Josh, and Ruth Rose looked back at the swan float as it slowly moved past them.

"Hey, where's the candy lady?" one of the kids behind Dink called out.

"Where is she?" asked Ruth Rose. "Where's Miss Chinatown?"

No one was standing behind the swan's head tossing candy.

Miss Chinatown had disappeared.

CHAPTER 5

"Where did she go?" Josh asked.

"Where did who go?" said a voice behind the kids.

It was Holden. He was out of breath, as if he'd been running.

"I had to make a porta-potty call," he said. "Did Miss Chinatown take off her mask yet?"

"She's not on the float!" Ruth Rose said. "She's gone!"

Holden looked confused. "What?"

"Look," Josh said. He tugged Holden's arm to bring him closer to the fence.

"Miss Chinatown was there throwing candy, then after the fireworks, she was gone. Just like that!"

Holden stared at the swan float. Suddenly he vaulted over the fence and raced after the float.

Dink, Josh, and Ruth Rose watched him run to the front of the truck cab and wave his arms. The truck stopped, and the driver's door opened. A woman wearing denim coveralls stepped out and began yelling at Holden.

By now the crowd around the kids had noticed that something was wrong. Dink heard voices saying, "What's going on?"

"Where's Miss Chinatown?"

"What's that guy doing in front of the float?"

There were dozens of other floats behind the swan float, all waiting for the parade to continue. Drivers were

stepping out of their trucks. Some were tooting their horns, as if this were an ordinary traffic jam.

People in the crowd began to get upset. Some guy yelled, "This is a bogus parade!"

A little kid asked, "Isn't there any more candy?"

Another kid answered, "Duh, Billy, the candy lady took off!"

Dink suddenly remembered something Holden had told them earlier. He said he hadn't heard from Lily in two days. No phone calls, no text messages. He had said he was worried about her. Now she was gone—or at least Miss Chinatown was gone.

"Come on, guys," Ruth Rose said. She grabbed the top of the fence, wedged one sneaker toe against it, and threw her other leg over.

"What're you doing?" Dink asked.

"We're supposed to stay with Holden," Ruth Rose said. "Besides, I'm not missing this!" She pulled her other leg over the top of the fence, then dropped to the ground on the other side.

"Me either!" Josh said. He followed Ruth Rose over the fence.

Dink watched his two friends run toward the swan float. Gulping a deep breath, he followed them.

When Dink reached the float, Holden and the truck driver had stopped yelling at each other. Dink joined Josh and Ruth Rose, who were standing behind Holden.

"I didn't see Miss Chinatown at all," the driver was telling Holden. "I was just watching the road in front of me. I don't know anything about whatever happened behind me!"

Just then two police officers approached. "What're you kids doing inside

the fence?" one of them asked. A name tag on his uniform jacket said OFFICER GOODMAN.

"We came to help our friend," Dink said, pointing at Holden.

"They're with me," Holden said.

"Yeah? And who are you?" the other officer asked Holden. Her name tag read OFFICER FEIST. "And what're you doing here? That fence is meant to keep folks out!"

"Um, I'm Holden Wong," Holden said. "I'm looking for my girlfriend, Lily. She was—"

"WHAT IS GOING ON HERE!" an angry voice interrupted. "THIS PARADE MUST PROCEED! WHY HAVE YOU STOPPED THE FLOAT?"

Dink jumped at the loud voice. He turned to see a man storming up to the group. He wore a suit the color of vanilla ice cream. His white hair was

swept back off his forehead. He had a thin white mustache and a red face. His dark eyes flashed anger as he charged toward the float.

"Excuse me, sir," Officer Goodman said. "Who are you?"

The man glared at Officer Goodman. He took a deep breath and closed his eyes for a second. "Dr. Winston Worthington," he said finally. "I am the parade manager. Now please answer my question! Under whose authority did you stop this float?"

Dink looked up at the angry man's red face. A blood vessel in his forehead was bulging, like a small snake under the skin. Dr. Worthington's eyes darted around the group, looking for someone to blame. His hands had formed into fists.

Dink knew he'd never seen this man before, but somehow he looked familiar.

"Um, I stopped the float," Holden said. "My girl—"

"And you are?" Dr. Worthington asked.

Officer Feist stepped forward. "Sir, Miss Chinatown has disappeared off the float," she said. "This young man thinks it was his girlfriend." She looked at Holden. "What's her name?"

"Lily Chen," Holden said. "She—"

"Miss Chinatown disappeared?" Dr. Worthington interrupted. His red face turned pale. "But that's impossible!" He turned to the float driver. "How do we get up on this thing?"

"Easy peasy," the driver said. "There's a ladder." She walked to the opposite side of the float. A small ladder was attached to the truck. It was partly hidden in blue flowers, and so narrow only a small person could climb its rungs.

"I'm not climbing that silly thing!" Dr. Worthington said. "There must be

another way. How do the workers get up and down?"

"There's a ramp in the back," the driver said. "This truck hauls freight when it's not used for parades. Come on, I'll show you."

The woman hurried to the back of the float and unhooked a rear section of the truck's bed. It made a ramp, which the driver lowered to the road.

Dr. Worthington marched up the ramp, quickly followed by the two police officers and Holden.

"Come on, guys!" Ruth Rose whispered. Following her lead, Dink and Josh clambered up the ramp. They all stood in the middle of the huge swan. Its wings spread above them, completely covered in white flower blossoms. The thousands of blossoms gave off a thick, sweet smell.

"She was right here!" Holden said.

He took a step forward. "Lily's not very tall. She must have stood on that box so we could see her."

Something crackled under Holden's foot. Dink looked down and saw wrapped candies scattered on the floor. Just behind the swan's neck stood a wooden box the size of a large toy chest.

"Well, I can see that she's not here, but how did she get off the float?" Officer

Goodman asked. "I mean, nobody saw her climb down that ladder, right?"

"She wouldn't just leave," Holden said. "Someone must have taken her!"

"But who? She was alone on the float, right?" Officer Feist asked.

"Enough talking!" Dr. Worthington spluttered. "Can we just get my parade moving again?"

"Sir, we have a situation here,"

Officer Goodman said. "Once we figure out what's going on, the parade will continue."

Dink felt Ruth Rose nudge his arm.

"Look," she murmured in his ear, and pointed toward the floor.

Dink looked. He saw only the box and a bunch of wrapped candies.

Then he noticed something else. A piece of black silk was sticking out from under the box. Dink recognized the sash. The last time he'd seen it, the sash had been tied around Miss Chinatown's waist.

CHAPTER 6

Dink and Ruth Rose moved at the same time. They grabbed the edges of the box and lifted it aside. A small figure wearing a golden robe lay on the floor. The candy purse had been pulled over her head. The black sash was tied around her wrists.

"Lily!" Holden yelled. He leaped forward, but the two police officers grabbed his arms and stopped him.

"Let us, Mr. Wong!" Officer Feist said.

The two officers knelt next to the

girl. One of them removed the bag from her head. Her eyes were closed. Shiny black hair had fallen over her face. They untied her hands.

"Is this Miss Chen?" Officer Feist asked Holden.

Holden stood with Dink, Josh, and Ruth Rose. His arm touched Dink's shoulder, and Dink could feel him trembling under his white sweater. "Yes," he said. "Is she okay?"

Lily opened her eyes. She looked around at the group. Dink could tell she was frightened.

The officers helped her sit up. She looked at Holden and smiled.

"Miss Chen, are you all right?" Officer Feist asked.

Lily nodded. "I'm okay," she said.

"Can you tell us what happened?" Officer Goodman asked.

"The crown is gone!" Dr. Worthington shouted. "Where is the ruby? I am responsible—"

"Please, sir," Officer Feist said, looking up at Dr. Worthington over her shoulder. "We'll handle this."

Suddenly Dr. Worthington stopped yelling. He brushed past Dink to the edge of the float. Dink watched him stare into the night, as if his mind was a thousand miles away. His face was no longer angry. It was blank.

"He took the crown," Lily said. "The man who grabbed me."

Everyone except Dr. Worthington was watching Lily. She pushed her hair out of her face and sat up straighter.

"I was standing on the box, throwing candy," she said. "Then I heard fireworks, and I was confused. We already had the fireworks before the dragon started

walking. So I just looked up at them like everyone else. Suddenly someone climbed over the side of the float."

She pointed to the top of the ladder. "It was a man wearing a dragon mask," she went on. "He pulled me down on the floor and took off my mask. Then he sprayed something in my face. It was awful, and it hurt my eyes. I felt him pull the crown off me. Then he put the bag over my head. I . . . I don't remember anything after that."

Dink's mind flashed back a half hour. They were all watching the dragon "walking" along the parade route. One of the pairs of legs crawled out from under the dragon and hurried away in the other direction. Toward the swan float.

"Um, I think I saw him," Dink said.

Everyone looked at him.

"You saw who attacked Miss Chen?" Officer Feist said.

Just then another police officer thudded up the ramp and into the middle of the swan float. "What's going on?" he asked the two officers.

They explained the situation.

"Okay," he said, "but let's finish this at the station. There are a few thousand unhappy people out there, and they want their parade!"

"We have to go to the police station, too?" Josh asked.

"That's right, son," the officer said. "Where are your parents?"

"My dad's back at our hotel," Dink said. "We're staying at the Bayside."

"You'd better call him," Ruth Rose said.

Everyone started to leave the float. Dink noticed that Holden and Lily each had a police escort. Dr. Worthington

walked alone, but the third officer was keeping an eye on him. One by one, they walked down the ramp.

"Let's take the easy-peasy way," Josh whispered to Dink.

"He means the ladder," Ruth Rose said.

Dink was standing next to the ladder's top rung, where it came up the side of the truck bed. He put his hands on the ladder and looked down. They were about six feet off the road. Flower blossoms partly covered the ladder rungs. It looked slippery.

"I'll take the ramp," he told Josh and Ruth Rose. But his fingers had touched something soft on the top rung. He looked and saw a piece of white yarn.

Dink pulled the yarn off the rung and examined it closely. Under the lights, it looked curly and silky. Dink thought of the yarn his mother used when she knit

scarves and sweaters every winter.

He had seen a white sweater only minutes ago, on Holden.

Dink slipped the yarn into his pocket and pulled out his cell phone. He hit speed dial for his father's number.

CHAPTER 7

A half hour later Dink, Josh, and Ruth Rose were sitting around a table in a small room at the police station. The floor was gray concrete. The walls were painted the color of pea soup. There were no windows.

Dink's father stood behind them. He shook his head and smiled at the three kids. "I never expected to be invited to a police station tonight," Mr. Duncan said.

"Sorry, Dad," Dink said. "We never expected someone to rob Miss Chinatown's crown!"

Officer Feist walked into the room. She carried a small tape recorder, which she set on the table.

"This won't take long," she said, turning on the machine. "I just want to record your statement about the man you saw running toward the swan float, Donald." She placed a pencil and notebook on the table next to the recorder.

Josh giggled. "We call him Dink," he said. "Or Dinkus."

Officer Feist grinned. "And what do we call you?" she asked.

"Josh."

"Joshua, actually," Ruth Rose said. She nudged Dink's arm.

"Don— I mean Dink, tell me what you saw," Officer Feist said.

"We were watching the dragon," Dink told her and the tape recorder. "You know how all those people were

underneath, carrying it along. Some of them were fooling around, running up and putting their heads inside the dragon's mouth. Well, one of them left. He—well, it could have been a she, I guess—anyway, this person came out from under the dragon and ran toward

the back. He or she wasn't very tall, I remember."

"So this person could have been a small man or woman, or a kid?" Officer Feist asked. "Exactly how big was this person?"

"Like Josh," Dink said. He nodded at his friend. "Skinny legs, too."

Officer Feist looked at Josh. "Would you stand up, please, Joshua?"

Josh stood up.

"How tall are you, Joshua?" Officer Feist asked.

"Almost five feet," Josh said. He tried to stand taller.

"How was this person dressed?" Officer Feist asked Dink.

Dink closed his eyes. He saw the dragon and the hundred pairs of red legs. "Well, everyone under the dragon was wearing red pants," he told Officer Feist. "But the person I saw had on a

sweater, too. It looked white or yellow under the light. I . . ."

Suddenly Dink stopped. Maybe the yarn in his pocket hadn't come from Holden's sweater! There were two white sweaters! He pulled it out of his pocket and placed it on the table. He explained where he'd found it.

"Do you think the guy who stole the crown left this behind?" Dink asked.

Officer Feist poked at the snippet of yarn with her pencil.

"There are lots of ways this could have gotten there," she said. "Dozens of people climbed that ladder when they were decorating the float." She smiled. "In fact, I have a sweater in my closet that this could have come from."

"But it could also have come from the person Dink saw, right?" Dink's father asked.

Officer Feist nodded. "That's right,

Mr. Duncan." She opened a drawer in the table and took out a small see-through evidence bag. Using the tip of her pencil, she pushed the yarn into the bag and sealed it. They all watched her write something on the outside of the bag.

"All of the people who carried the dragon are being searched and questioned right now," Officer Feist said. "The floats and the dragon have been returned to the warehouse. They'll be kept there under police guard until we get to the bottom of this."

"Will you try to match the yarn I found with what they're wearing?" Dink asked.

"Absolutely," Officer Feist said. "I'll have one of my detectives run it over immediately after this interview." She pushed the OFF button on the tape recorder. "When are you folks planning to return to Connecticut?"

"Day after tomorrow," Dink's father said. "Tuesday. Will that be a problem?"

Officer Feist opened her notebook and made a note. "I'll call you tomorrow," she said. "But I don't think you'll need to change your travel plans."

She stood up. "Now you can all go to your hotel and get a good night's sleep," she said.

Officer Feist held the door open. Dink's father left first, with Josh and Ruth Rose right behind. Dink followed them all down a long hallway.

"Dink!" someone called out. Holden came out of a room on Dink's right. He was escorted by two police officers Dink hadn't seen before. Each held one of Holden's arms.

Holden's black hair was messed up. His eyes were red and swollen. "They've got Lily!" Holden cried. "Tell them we didn't steal anything!"

Josh, Ruth Rose, and Dink's father all turned back to stare.

Dink stopped in his tracks, stunned. Holden and Lily were being arrested!

The officers marched Holden past Dink and around a corner in the hallway.

Dink hurried to catch up to his father, Josh, and Ruth Rose. He passed another room, where he heard crying.

He looked through the open door and gasped.

At a small table, Lily sat between an older Chinese man and woman. Dink figured they were Lily's parents. The couple sat as still as statues, staring at their daughter.

Lily was sobbing as Officer Goodman placed handcuffs around her slim wrists.

CHAPTER 8

It was dark outside the police station, so Dink's father stopped a cab and they all got in. Dink sat in the back, between Josh and Ruth Rose. His father sat next to the driver.

"Do you think they did it?" Josh whispered to Dink and Ruth Rose.

"But Lily was tied up with that sash thing," Ruth Rose said. "And she had that bag over her head."

"Maybe the cops think Holden tied her, to make it look like someone else did it," Josh said.

Dink remembered the few minutes that Holden had disappeared during the parade. He'd told the kids that he'd gone to use one of the portable bathrooms. Had he been lying?

Dink also remembered the look on Holden's face when they found Lily tied up. That look was no lie!

"I believe Holden," Dink said. "Did you see his face when we found Lily hidden under that box? He was really shocked, guys."

The cabdriver pulled up in front of the Bayside Hotel. Dink's father paid him, and they all went inside. The concierge, Mr. Alderson, smiled from behind his desk.

"Good evening, folks," he said. "How was your day, kids?"

"Fine, thank you," they all murmured. No one wanted to mention what happened at the parade.

The elevator took them to the third floor. The Bayside was the kind of hotel that offered its guests small apartments as well as single rooms. Dink's father had rented an apartment with three bedrooms, a living room, and a tiny kitchen.

Josh opened the refrigerator. "There's nothing to eat," he announced.

"What would you like, Josh?" Mr. Duncan asked. He winked at Dink and Ruth Rose behind Josh's back. "A juicy steak with mashed potatoes? Fried chicken? Spaghetti and meatballs?"

"Yes!" Josh said, grinning at the others. He threw himself on the sofa and picked up his sketchbook.

"I heard some of what you kids said in the cab," Dink's father said. "Do you really think Holden and his girlfriend stole the crown?"

"It would have been pretty easy,"

Josh said. "He and Lily could have cooked it all up together. There were so many people, and all those fireworks going off. Holden could have climbed into the float with Lily, and they could have faked the robbery."

"But what if Lily hadn't been chosen as Miss Chinatown?" Ruth Rose asked. "What if the other girl was chosen?"

"Then they could have robbed the crown off her head instead!" Josh said. "Only it *was* Lily, so their plan was perfect."

"I don't know," Dink's father said. "Holden seems like a decent kid."

"I agree with you, Dad," Dink said. "Plus, he was so surprised that she was under that box. How could he fake that?"

"Don't forget he's studying acting in college," Ruth Rose reminded them. "Maybe he was only pretending to be surprised."

"But what about that person I saw running away from the dragon?" Dink asked. "And heading right for the swan float?"

No one had an answer. The four sat and thought. Josh turned pages in his sketchbook and picked up his pencil.

"Dad, can we help Holden and Lily?" Dink asked his father after a moment. "I mean, is there anything we can do?"

Dink's father stood up. "I don't know, son," he said. "But I'll call the police station. Maybe I can help Holden and Lily get a lawyer. After all, I hired Holden to take you kids to the parade."

Dink's father walked to his bedroom.

Ruth Rose scooted over next to Josh. "What're you drawing?" she asked.

"Just parade stuff," Josh said.

"Can I look?" Ruth Rose asked.

"Sure, Nosy Rosy," Josh teased. He tilted the sketchbook so she could see.

"Josh, these are so good!" Ruth Rose said. "Look, Dink!"

Dink stood behind the sofa and looked over Ruth Rose's shoulder. Josh had made several small drawings on one of the pages. One was a man's face that Dink thought was supposed to be Dr. Worthington. Josh had also made sketches of two sea lions, the dragon's head, and Holden's Green Machine. Dink smiled at the three small figures sitting in the passenger seat. It was Josh, Ruth Rose, and himself.

At the bottom of the page, Josh was drawing what looked like some kind of flying animal. It was a sort of furry box with wings.

"What's that?" Dink asked.

"It's supposed to be the swan float," Josh said. "But it's not finished."

Ruth Rose giggled. "With curly hair?" she asked.

"Duh, that's not hair," Josh said. "Those are the flowers on the float!" He made a few marks with his pencil. "Here are the swan's wings, and here's Miss Chinatown throwing candy, and here's—"

"Wait a minute!" Dink cried. He jumped over the back of the sofa, landing

next to Josh. He grabbed the sketchbook and pointed to the drawing. "This looks like the same picture that guy at the aquarium was drawing on his laptop!"

Dink plucked Josh's pencil from his friend's fingers. He made a few lines on the side of Josh's rectangle. "See, that guy's drawing had these lines, too. I think they were meant to be that little ladder on the side of the float."

"Why would some stranger be drawing the swan float?" Ruth Rose asked.

Just then Dink's father came into the room. "I have some bad news," he said. "The police searched Holden's apartment and his Green Machine bike. They found the crown. It was hidden inside a compartment under the passenger seat on Holden's bike."

The three kids sat with their mouths open. No one said a word. Traffic hummed outside. The wall clock ticked. Dink felt his heart racing.

"Did they find the ruby?" Dink asked.

His father shook his head. "The ruby had been removed from the crown," he said. "Both Lily and Holden have been arrested and charged with the theft."

CHAPTER 9

Dink felt sick to his stomach. The more he thought about it, the more convinced he became that someone else, not Holden and Lily, had stolen the ruby. And that someone was trying to make Holden and Lily look guilty.

Dink's mind went back to the guy with the laptop inside the aquarium. Why had he been drawing a computer picture of the swan float? Unless he knew that Miss Chinatown would be wearing a priceless ruby in her crown and he planned to steal it? Geez, had Dink been sitting right next to the thief?

Dink told the others what he was thinking. "I have a funny feeling about that guy," he said.

"And I have a funny feeling about the person you saw running from the dragon," Dink's father said. "Maybe he's our crook."

"I just thought of something," Ruth Rose said. "Remember what Lily said about the fireworks? She said she was surprised when the second fireworks went off. She told us that everyone looked up toward the sky, and that's when the guy jumped into the float and sprayed something in her face."

Ruth Rose sat up straight. "Do you think someone set off the second fireworks so people would take their eyes off Miss Chinatown?" she asked.

"Oh my gosh!" Dink said. "The

second fireworks! I'm so dumb! The guy in the aquarium was talking on his cell phone after we sat down. I thought I heard him say 'the second tire works,' but now I think what he really said was 'the second fireworks'! It all makes sense. That guy was planning the robbery with whoever he had on the phone! And the drawing of the swan float on his laptop was part of the plan!"

Ruth Rose said, "So he was telling someone to snatch the crown off Lily during the second fireworks, when everyone was looking up at the sky, not at her! And that someone might have been the person we saw leaving the dragon and running toward the swan float!"

"But what about the cops finding the crown in Holden's buggy?" Josh asked.

"It could have been put there by the real crooks," Dink said. "To make it look like Holden had hidden it."

"That would mean that the crooks knew Holden had such a buggy," Dink's father said. "And where to find it after they took the crown."

"Right," Dink said. "It would have been easy to find Holden. He drives that thing all over town! He even has a website with a picture of his bike!"

"And now Holden and Lily are in jail," Josh said.

"Did you get them a lawyer?" Dink asked his father.

"I didn't need to," Mr. Duncan said. "Lily's parents wanted to call their own attorney. He arrives tomorrow morning."

"So they have to stay in jail?" Ruth Rose asked. "That's not fair!"

Dink's father sighed. "No, it doesn't seem fair," he said. "But don't forget that a valuable ruby has been stolen. And even if we think Holden is innocent, the

crown was found in his bike. The police seem to think that's enough to charge Holden with the crime."

"But the police don't know Holden," Ruth Rose said. "We do, and we think he's innocent!"

"Well, we might be able to prove that Holden is innocent," Dink's father went on, "if we can prove that someone else is guilty." He looked at his watch. "But now it's time for bed, kiddos. There's nothing we can do tonight."

A half hour later, Dink lay in his bed staring at the dark ceiling. Josh was across the room in the other bed, lightly snoring. Nothing could keep him awake!

"Prove that someone else is guilty," Dink's father had said. *Then that's what we'll do!* Dink decided. *But how? We need a plan!*

Dink climbed out of bed and opened

the door. Across the hall, he saw a strip of light under Ruth Rose's door. *She must be reading,* he thought.

Dink tapped lightly on her door. She opened it, wearing yellow pajamas with blue kangaroos jumping all over the flannel. "Are you awake?" Dink whispered.

Ruth Rose grinned. "No, I'm asleep," she said. "What's going on?"

"Can I come in?" Dink whispered. "I don't want to wake my dad."

"Sure." Ruth Rose let Dink in. "Where's Josh?"

"Right here!" Josh said, stumbling into the room. His hair was a mess and he was rubbing sleep out of his eyes. "What's up?"

The kids grabbed pillows off the twin beds and sat on the rug.

"Do we agree that Holden and Lily didn't steal that ruby?" Dink asked.

"I do!" Ruth Rose said.

They both looked at Josh. His mouth was open in a huge yawn.

Josh looked back at them, blinking. "Okay, I guess I go along with you," he said. "But what about the crown the cops found in Holden's buggy?"

"Josh," Ruth Rose said, "if Holden stole the crown, why would he hide it in his own bike? That would be pretty dumb, and Holden isn't dumb! Somebody else must have put it there, knowing the cops would search."

"Okay, we agree," Dink said. "Now we just have to find the real crook."

"Except for one teeny-tiny thing," Josh said. "We don't know who it is."

"I have one idea," Dink said. "That guy with the laptop at the aquarium."

"Yeah, you said he had a drawing of the swan float on his computer," Ruth Rose said.

"Well, I think it was the swan float," Dink said.

"So how do we find this guy?" Josh asked. "He could be anywhere."

"I don't know," Dink said. "If you just stole a priceless ruby, what would you do?"

"Well, I wouldn't try to sell it," Ruth Rose said. "The theft will be all over the newspapers and TV by tomorrow morning. It's probably on the Internet right now!"

"Know what I'd do?" asked Josh. "I'd hop a plane. No, I'd buy a boat and sail around the world!"

A picture of a sailboat flashed into Dink's mind. Where had he seen a sailboat? Then he knew.

Dink threw a pillow at Josh. "You're a genius!" he yelled.

"I am?" Josh asked. He blinked. "Cool!"

CHAPTER 10

"Why is Josh a genius?" Ruth Rose asked.

"Because he made me remember something about that guy in the aquarium," Dink said. "First, he had a dark tan. And he had this long knife, the kind guys who go fishing a lot carry on them. And when I saw him last, he was walking toward the docks at Fisherman's Wharf."

"I don't get it," Josh said.

"There are boats tied up to the docks," Dink said. "And a picture of a sailboat was the screen saver on his laptop. Guys, I think this guy keeps a

boat at Fisherman's Wharf!"

"So if we go back there, we might be able to find his boat?" Ruth Rose said. "Then we could find him!"

Dink nodded. "After we find him, we'll tell the police, and maybe they'll question him. At least they'll have another suspect!"

They heard a knock on Ruth Rose's door. "Enough chatting, you three night owls," Dink's father said. "Boys, get to bed, please."

"Okay, Dad!" Dink called. Then he whispered to Josh and Ruth Rose, "Tomorrow we find Mr. Laptop!"

The next morning Dink's father made oatmeal with raisins for himself and the kids. "I have meetings most of this morning," he told them. "I had asked Holden to take you to see the Golden Gate Bridge, but that's out now. Any plans?"

"We're going to try to prove Holden isn't the crook!" Dink said. Then he noticed the look on his father's face, a look he knew. "Don't worry, Dad, we won't do anything dangerous."

"And I won't be dragged back to the police station?" Mr. Duncan asked.

Dink shook his head. "Promise!" But to himself Dink said, *I hope not!*

"Oh, speaking of that, I had an early phone call from Officer Feist," Dink's father said. "No luck finding the ruby. They searched all one hundred people who were walking the dragon."

"Do they know which one I saw running toward the swan float?" Dink asked. "That could be the crook!"

"The police told me they'd love to talk to that person," Dink's father said. "But not one of the dragon carriers admitted to it. He or she cleverly kept the mask on."

"Are Holden and Lily still in jail?" Dink asked.

"Holden is," Mr. Duncan said. "Lily is underage, so the Chens' attorney convinced the police to let her go home. She can't leave her parents' house for any reason until the crime has been solved."

"Bummer," Josh said.

Dink's father looked at his watch. Then he took a fast sip of coffee and stood up. "Will you kids take care of these dishes?" he asked. "I have to jump on a cable car in ten minutes!"

Dink rinsed the bowls and spoons while Ruth Rose and Josh got ready to leave. With his hands in the water, Dink tried to remember details of the boat he'd seen on the man's laptop. It had been a sailboat, but that was all he could remember. Why hadn't he looked more closely at that screen saver?

Five minutes later they were in the elevator heading for the lobby. Dink's cell phone was in his pocket. Ruth Rose had her backpack. Knowing her, Dink was sure she'd have a Swiss Army knife, a camera, and at least one guidebook or map. Josh carried his sketchbook.

Mr. Alderson was arranging a stack of newspapers for hotel guests to grab on their way out. "Good morning, kids," he said. "Is your friend Mr. Wong picking you up in his green buggy?"

Dink just stared at the man. He wasn't sure how much he should say.

"No, he's being detained elsewhere," Josh piped up.

Dink stared at Josh. Detained? Dink figured Josh had heard that word on some TV show.

"Oh, then can I help you with transportation?" Mr. Alderson asked.

"Yes, how do we get to Fisherman's

Wharf from here?" Dink asked.

"That's an easy one," Mr. Alderson said. He unfolded a map and put his finger on a spot. "This is us, the Bayside Hotel." Then he moved his finger along streets until it rested at Fisherman's Wharf. "Walk outside, take a left, and go to the first corner. You'll see a brown and white sign. It's where the cable car stops. It will take you right to the wharf. It's about a twenty-minute ride."

"Thanks a lot!" Dink said. The kids headed for the door.

"Um, excuse me," Mr. Alderson said. "The cable cars are six dollars for each of you, I believe. Do you have passes?"

"I think Holden has them," Dink said.

Ruth Rose patted her backpack. "I have money," she said. "My parents told me San Francisco was expensive."

"No need to spend your money," Mr.

Alderson said. He pulled three passes from his desk and handed them to the kids. "These let you use any cable car or bus in the city. Have fun!"

"We will!" Dink said. They thanked him again, then hurried through the exit.

While they waited for the cable car, Ruth Rose checked her map. "Look, here's Pier 39," she said. "That's right next to the sea lions."

"Dude, how do we find this guy's boat?" Josh asked Dink.

"I have no clue, dude," Dink said as a cable car slowed at their stop.

CHAPTER 11

Ruth Rose showed the passes to the uniformed conductor, and they boarded the cable car. It rode along a track in the street, clanging its bell whenever they came to an intersection. It was too noisy and windy for talking, so the kids just hung on and watched the scenery go by. When the car plunged down the steep street, they all yelled.

"Twenty-two minutes," Ruth Rose said as the kids hopped off at Fisherman's Wharf. All of the other people on the car were headed in the same direction, so the

kids just followed along. Three minutes later they were in front of the aquarium.

The morning was cool and breezy. Dink could smell the sea lions, but the fog hid them from view. The kids walked closer to the water. Now they could see and hear the sea lions. The huge creatures were barking and flopping on top of each other on the docks. A few of them slipped into the water. Tourists posed for pictures with the sea lions in the background.

"There are the boats," Dink said. He pointed to several that were tied to the end of docks. Some were moored farther out in the water.

"But which one are we looking for?" Ruth Rose asked.

"It's a sailboat," Dink said. He tried to remember what he'd seen on that guy's laptop screen saver. "I think it was green . . . or blue."

"Great," Josh said. He flipped open his sketchbook. "Maybe this will help."

"What, you drew the boat?" Dink asked. "Josh, you're awesome!"

"I know I'm awesome, but I didn't draw the boat," Josh said. "I drew the guy we saw in the aquarium. If we can't find his boat, maybe we can find him."

He pointed to a drawing of a man's head. Dink looked at the small sketch. "But I thought this was Dr. Worthington," he said.

Josh shrugged. "Nope, this is the guy who was sitting at the table near us yesterday," he said. "Remember, he had an *M* tattooed on the back of each hand. Maybe M&M's are his favorite candy."

"Now I know why I thought Dr. Worthington looked familiar!" Dink cried. "He looks just like the laptop guy! They could be related."

"Dr. Worthington has white hair and

a skinny mustache," Ruth Rose said.
"The laptop guy is bald."

"Wait a sec." Josh pulled a pencil
from his pocket and added hair and a
mustache to the drawing.

"You're right," Ruth Rose said. "Now he looks just like Dr. Worthington!"

"It's pretty creepy if they're related to each other," Dink said. "One had a drawing of the swan float in his computer, and the other is the manager of the parade!"

"Maybe Dr. Worthington is a crook, too," Josh said.

"Do you remember how mad he was when the parade got stopped last night?" Ruth Rose asked.

Dink nodded. "Yeah, I do remember. But then when we found Lily and he knew the crown had been stolen, he stopped yelling. In fact, he looked kind of sad."

"How do we find the boat?" Josh asked. "We can't go out on the docks or the sea lions will gobble us up!"

"They eat fish, not tourists," Ruth Rose said. "But I have an idea. There

must be an office around here where they keep track of all the boats that come and go. We can show them Josh's picture of the guy we saw in the aquarium. If he keeps a boat here, they might know him."

"Great idea," Josh said. "Wait a minute." He erased the hair and mustache from his drawing.

"Give him a tan," Dink suggested.

Josh darkened the man's face. "How's that?"

"Perfect," Dink said. "It's Laptop Man again."

The kids walked around. The sun was getting brighter through the fog, but they didn't see anything that looked like an office for boaters.

"I have an idea," Ruth Rose said. "Wait here." She ran over to a guy selling balloons. Dink and Josh watched her talking to him. Then she ran back.

"The office is on the fuel dock," she told them. "That's where the boaters buy gas."

"Where's the fuel dock?" Dink asked.

Ruth Rose pointed. "Way at the end of that pier," she said. "He said the sea lions don't like the smell of gas, so they stay away."

The kids hiked to the pier. Some of the fog disappeared and the sun came out. At the end of the pier were two gas pumps outside a small white building. A sign on the door said HARBORMASTER.

Dink, Josh, and Ruth Rose opened the door and walked inside. The room was tiny and hot. Two men sat at desks, typing on computers. Both were in T-shirts.

Pictures of boats decorated the walls. A row of hooks held a few jackets and sweaters. A heater in the corner hummed and threw out too much warmth for such a small space.

"Help you?" one of the men asked. He had dark hair and a tanned face. The man didn't get up, just swiveled his chair around. The other man kept typing.

Dink's mind raced, searching for something to say. Why would three kids walk in asking about some guy whose name they didn't even know? Dink shot a look at Josh, who stood there holding his sketchbook.

"We're looking for someone," Dink said finally. "We, um, met him in the aquarium yesterday. He was working on a cool laptop. My dad wants to buy me one, so I was wondering if . . ." Dink felt his face go red.

"Here's his picture," Josh said, jumping in. "I draw everyone I meet." He thrust his sketchbook toward the man. "We think he has a boat here somewhere."

The man squinted, then took the sketchbook and showed it to his com-

panion. "Take a look, Burk," he said. "I don't recognize this dude."

The man named Burk glanced at Josh's drawing, then shook his head. "Nope, never saw him, either." He handed the sketchbook back to Josh. At the same time, Dink noticed the man take a quick look out the window. Then he went back to working at his computer.

Dink turned to see what Burk had been looking at. Through the window, Dink could see sun and blue sky. He also saw a green sailboat moored to a buoy.

CHAPTER 12

"Well, thanks a lot," Dink said to the two men. "My dad is waiting outside, so we'd better get going. He gets really mad when I'm late!"

Dink hustled Josh and Ruth Rose out the door.

"Okay, what's going on?" Josh asked. "Your dad doesn't even know where we are. And he never gets mad!"

"Follow me!" Dink said. He hurried toward the water, hoping the guy in the harbormaster shed wasn't watching. Dink stopped when they reached a short

dock. He stepped behind a row of tall blue recycling bins.

"That's the sailboat!" he said, pointing.

Josh and Ruth Rose just looked at him.

"The one I saw on that guy's laptop in the aquarium!" Dink added.

"How did you know it was here?" asked Ruth Rose.

"I caught that guy Burk sneaking a peek at it," Dink said. "After he told us he didn't recognize Josh's drawing, he looked right out the window at the boat."

The boat was moored about fifty yards out into the water. It was painted green, but some of the paint was chipped away. The sails were down, but Dink could see that they were dirty. Someone's T-shirt was pinned to a rope, flapping in the breeze. A rubber dinghy was tied to the aft end of the boat.

"I wonder if the laptop guy is out there," Josh said.

"I don't know," Dink said, wishing he had binoculars.

Just then they heard a door slam behind them. They looked and saw a man leaving the harbormaster shed. He was hurrying toward the dock.

"Duck!" Ruth Rose said. All three of them scrunched down behind the recycling bins.

The man called Burk rushed past them and hurried out onto the dock. He was wearing a light-colored fisherman's sweater. They watched him stop at the end of the dock.

Less than a minute later, a man on the sailboat stepped into the dinghy, untied the rope, and started the motor. It took only a minute or two to reach the end of the dock. He and Burk began talking. The dinghy driver remained seated in his boat with the motor running. Burk

stood on the dock, looking down at him. They both looked angry.

"The guy in the boat is Laptop Man!" Josh whispered to his two friends.

"I know," Dink answered, keeping his voice low. "And I think Burk is the man I saw last night, running toward the swan float."

"He's small enough to climb that little ladder," Ruth Rose said. "And I'll bet anything that piece of yarn you found came from his sweater!"

"Right," Dink said. "And when we saw the guy with the laptop at the aquarium, he was telling Burk to go to the swan float during the second fireworks. He even drew a picture for him. I'll bet you he emailed it."

"So let's arrest them!" Josh said.

"We can't prove they stole anything," Dink said. "And even if we could, we have to tell the police."

"Why don't we call them right now?" Ruth Rose asked. "You've got your cell phone, right?"

Dink looked at Ruth Rose. "What would we say?" he asked.

"We could tell them we found a guy wearing a sweater that matches that piece of yarn," Ruth Rose suggested.

"Guys, something is happening!" Josh whispered.

The man in the boat stood up. He reached into the pocket of his jeans and pulled out something small enough to conceal in one hand. He passed the object to Burk, who looked at it, then slipped it into his own pocket.

"What did he give him?" Josh asked.

"Could it be the ruby?" Ruth Rose asked. "There's our proof!"

"No, the ruby was bigger," Dink said. "It's about the size of an apple. And if Burk stole the ruby last night and gave it

to Laptop Guy, why would he be giving
it back to Burk now?"

The man in the dinghy shoved off,
heading out toward his sailboat. Burk
turned and walked back the way he'd
come. He passed within two feet of

the recycling bins where the kids were hiding.

"He doesn't look happy," Ruth Rose said.

They watched him approach the harbormaster shed. But he didn't go in. He kept walking toward the street.

"Where's he going?" Josh asked.

"I don't know, but wherever it is, we're going, too!" Dink said.

CHAPTER 13

The kids let Burk get about a hundred yards ahead of them, then they followed. Away from the water, the fog was thicker, making it difficult to see him.

Burk stopped at a street corner. He glanced at his watch, then looked around as if waiting for someone.

"What's he doing?" Josh asked.

The kids were huddled next to a small food store that sold sandwiches. Delicious smells came through the open window.

Burk looked at his watch again, then leaned against a sign.

"Oh my gosh, look!" Ruth Rose said.

The sign Burk was leaning on said CABLE CAR STOP.

"He's gonna get on a cable car!" Josh said.

Just then they heard a rattling noise. A cable car was headed down the street, slowing. Burk raised an arm, and the car stopped. They saw him leap on.

"We have to get on, too!" Dink said. "Let's go!"

"But he'll see us!" Josh said.

"Not if we get on the back," Dink said. "See, there's a little platform. Run!"

The kids sprinted and jumped onto the cable car just as it began moving. The car was crowded, and they hid behind a bunch of tourists with cameras and maps clutched in their hands.

"Can you see him, Josh?" Dink asked.

Josh was the tallest of the three. Standing on tiptoes, he peeked from

behind his sketchbook over the heads of the tourists. "He's standing right by the front door," he said.

The car sped along, swerving and clattering as the underground cable pulled it up the hill along its route. It stopped twice for new passengers. When

the car stopped a third time, the group of tourists clambered off, talking in a language the kids didn't understand.

"He's getting off, too!" Josh whispered.

The kids hopped off the rear of the car, keeping their eyes on Burk's back as he headed into the fog.

"Where the heck are we?" Josh asked.

"I think I know," Ruth Rose said. She bent over and picked up something. "Look at this." She was holding a flower blossom.

"This is where the parade was last night!" Dink said.

"Look at the ground," Ruth Rose said. "There are blossoms everywhere. They fell off the floats."

Burk walked slowly through the fog. The kids followed him, their footsteps muffled by the dampness.

He stopped in front of a building the

size of Dink's school back home—it was the warehouse where they'd seen the dragon!

"What's he doing?" Dink asked.

Burk had walked up to the door. The kids watched him pull something from his pocket. They heard a click, then a rattling noise.

"That sounded like a lock," Ruth Rose said.

"Yeah, and I'll bet Dink's Laptop Guy gave him the key," Josh said.

Burk disappeared inside the building.

"Come on," Dink said.

Dink, Josh, and Ruth Rose scurried quietly to the door. An open padlock dangled from a hasp.

The kids peered into the building. The floats sat in the darkness like sleeping giants. On top of the closest truck bed, Dink saw an oversized tiger, crouching in a jungle setting. He could smell the

flowers that made up the tiger's orange and black body.

"This is where they keep the floats," Josh whispered.

Along one wall lay the dragon. Its two-hundred-foot length was only partly visible in the dim light. Dink thought it looked asleep. He had liked the dragon better when it was dancing along in the parade.

"This place is creeping me out," Josh said.

The three kids stepped inside. Josh pulled the door partly closed behind them. He folded his sketchbook and used it to wedge the door open a couple of inches.

"What're you doing?" Dink whispered.

"I hate dark places," Josh said. "My pad will let in a little light."

They stood to let their eyes adjust. Looking around, Dink saw no windows. Then he felt a hand grab his arm. Ruth

Rose pulled Dink down and whispered in his ear, "Look over by the dragon. I think I saw a light."

Tiptoeing, the kids headed toward that side of the massive space. As they drew closer, they could see Burk crouched by the dragon's head. In one hand, he held a flashlight. The other hand was inside the dragon's mouth.

"What's he—"

Dink stopped Josh from speaking. As quietly as possible, he drew his cell phone from his pocket. Getting down on his knees, Dink crawled toward the dragon. When he was as close as he dared go, he aimed the phone's camera lens at Burk's back.

Burk pulled something from the dragon's mouth. It was a round object, the size of a tennis ball. He turned his light on the object and it blazed red. It was the ruby.

Grinning, Dink pushed the button on his cell-phone camera. It made a quiet clicking noise.

Burk lurched around. "What the . . ." Leaping to his feet, he bolted toward Dink.

"Run!" Ruth Rose screamed.

"Split up!" Josh yelled.

Dink raced for the nearest float, shoving his cell phone into a pocket. He nearly bumped into the float. Looking up, he saw the tiger leering down at him. Dink crawled under the truck bed and made himself as small as he could behind one of the rear tires.

Some of the flowers and vines that made the tiger's "jungle" hung down over the sides of the truck. Dink felt hidden, but he knew Burk could find him with his flashlight. He wondered where Josh and Ruth Rose were hiding.

Suddenly an earsplitting whistle

pierced the air. "POLICE! FREEZE!" a
voice shouted.

Dink peered out from under the
truck. If the police were here, he was
getting out of this place right now!
He sprinted for the door as fast as his
trembling legs would take him.

Somebody grabbed him as soon as he had cleared the door. It was Josh, who pulled Dink out of the way.

Then Ruth Rose slammed the door shut and snapped the padlock. She turned and grinned at Dink. "Josh and I made a plan when you went to take the guy's picture," she said.

"But . . . but the police, the whistle . . . ," Dink stammered.

Ruth Rose held up her Swiss Army knife. From it dangled a tiny teddy bear and a shiny police whistle. "That was me," she said. "I was hoping Burk would think I was the police and hide, and you'd run outside." She dropped her knife into her backpack. "And you did!"

Josh picked up his bent sketchbook. "Now use that cell phone of yours and call the real police!" he said.

CHAPTER 14

"They're twin brothers?" Dink asked.

Dink, Josh, and Ruth Rose were sitting on the floor in the living room of their Bayside Hotel apartment. Dink's father sat on the sofa. He had just gotten off the phone with Officer Feist.

"Yes, Dr. Winston Worthington has a twin brother named Wayne Worthington," Dink's father told them. "Wayne got out of prison a few months ago. He stayed with Winston for a while, then borrowed some money from him and bought that old sailboat, where he now lives."

Dink thought about Wayne's tattoos. "So those were *W*'s on his hands, not *M*'s," he said. "I was reading them upside down!"

His father nodded. "Apparently, Wayne did some snooping when his brother wasn't around," he went on. "That's how he learned about the parade, Miss Chinatown's crown, even when the fireworks would go off. He was the one who set off the second round of fireworks."

"So he decided to steal the ruby?" asked Ruth Rose.

"Yes, but he needed help, so he enlisted Burk, the little guy who actually stole the crown right off Lily's head," Dink's father said. "He and Burk had once shared a prison cell."

"So that's why Dr. Worthington seemed so sad on the swan float," Dink said. "He must have figured out that his own brother was the crook!"

"I think you're right about that," Mr. Duncan said. "Luckily, you kids figured out what they were up to."

"Dad, why didn't Burk just take off with the ruby after he stole it?" Dink asked. "Why did he hide it in the dragon's mouth?"

"Burk knew if he didn't go back to help carry the dragon in the parade, he would be suspected," Dink's father answered. "But he was worried that everyone would be searched, so he stuck the ruby in the dragon's mouth, figuring he or his partner in crime could get it later."

"So he confessed?" Ruth Rose asked.

Dink's father laughed. "Yes, he did," he said. "But not right away. When the cops let Burk out of the warehouse, he denied everything. Said there was no proof. But when the police showed him

the picture Dink took, he changed his story."

"Cool!" Dink said. "I wasn't sure if the picture was any good. It came out pretty dark."

"It was fine," his father said. "It showed Burk holding the ruby. And when the piece of yarn matched his sweater exactly, he began to sing like a bird."

"Did Burk put the crown in Holden's buggy?" Dink asked.

"Yes, because he hoped that would make the police believe that Holden and his girlfriend had pulled off the caper," Dink's father said. "While Wayne was staying with his brother, he learned that Lily was one of the two finalists for Miss Chinatown. So he followed her, learned about Holden, then made his plans."

"But that was pretty dumb," Ruth Rose said. "Because even if Holden was the thief, he would never have hidden the crown in his own buggy!"

Dink's father laughed again. "That's right," he said. "But most crooks aren't very smart!"

"So where are Holden and Lily?" Josh asked. "I hope he's not still in jail!"

Just then the apartment telephone rang. Dink's father answered. "Yes, please send them up, Mr. Alderson," he said into the phone.

"Send what up?" Dink asked.

"I ordered take-out food," his father said.

A minute later there was a knock on the door. Dink got up and opened it. Holden and Lily stepped in, with bags that smelled very good.

"Is anyone here hungry?" Holden asked.

"Yes!" everyone yelled.

Dear Readers,

If someone asked you to name your favorite thing, what would you say? Chocolate? Money? Reading? Watching TV? Playing a sport? Obviously, this list could go on and on. If you were to ask me, I would have to admit that I like all the things in the above list, but my favorite thing is traveling. I have been many places in the United States, and have visited a lot of other countries as well. Here's just part of my travel list in the U.S.: Hawaii, Florida, California, Colorado, Texas, Washington State and Washington, D.C., Maine, Rhode Island, and Pennsylvania. I have also had wonderful vacations in England, France, Italy, Hong Kong, Panama, Belize, Germany, Mexico, Canada, and India.

In *The New Year Dragon Dilemma*, my

characters travel to one of my favorite cities: San Francisco, California. Have you been there? What a place! My first visit to San Francisco was during a college vacation. I'll never forget the steep hills, the cable cars, the food, and the smells and noises made by those sea lions at Fisherman's Wharf. And I love to eat Chinese food, so I loved wandering around Chinatown.

It's not hard to find a mystery in a large city. You just have to use your imagination and keep your eyes open. In this book, Dink, Josh, and Ruth Rose had a lot of fun in San Francisco. But they found a crime to solve, too. I hope you enjoyed going along with them on their big adventure!

Happy reading!

Sincerely,

Ron Roy

P.S. Be sure to look for the answer to the hidden message on the bottom of the next page. And please keep visiting my website at ronroy.com!

Did you find the secret message hidden in this book?

If you *don't* want to know the answer, *don't* look at the bottom of this page!

Answer:
GUM LUNG ROARS
SEE YOU NEXT YEAR

Calendar Mysteries

Help Bradley, Brian, Lucy, and Nate . . .

. . . solve a mystery a month!